MOUNTAIN STARS PRESS
WYOMING • USA

For the rowdy adventurers with dreams of greatness
—C.D.R. and Z.P.

Mountain Stars Press
caseyrislovbooks@gmail.com
www.caseyrislovbooks.com

Printed in China
First Edition
10 9 8 7 6 5 4 3 2 1
LCCN on file
ISBN 978-0-578-29442-1

This book was proudly produced by Book Bridge Press • www.bookbridgepress.com

Can you find all the animals in the book?

Badger	Horse
Beaver	Hummingbird
Bison	Ladybug
Black-footed ferret	Mouse
Chipmunk	Owl
Cricket	Pika
Deer	Prairie dog
Duck	Praying mantis
Dung beetle	Rabbit
Elk	Raven
Falcon	Salamander
Fox	Spider
Frog	Squirrel
Goose	Western meadowlark
Grasshopper	Woodpecker

Way out West
in the morning's bright sun,
Rowdy Randy was alert
and busy as always.

The horsefly had made quite a name for herself
in the West as a stubborn lone ranger,
a gutsy cowgirl who worked better alone.

But today was different.

Today there was buzzing, cooing, and chatter
as Rowdy Randy was deciding who would be
in her great western show.

"It takes a confident cowgirl
to recognize the talents of others,"
she admitted.

Creatures from every rock, den, and tree
came her way to audition for her show.
The contestants saddled up to
demonstrate that they too had guts and grit,
just like the legend.

The event would take place in the middle of
Nowhere Territory. The outlaw
cast and crew were already working and
practicing their parts. They'd need to work hard
to be worth remembering.

The brown, paddle-tailed water varmints created benches
by the bunches. The eight-legged crawlers set up the high jump and
tightrope events. Chirping virtuosos practiced their nightly tunes.

Refreshment stands and stage props
were being constructed. The chatty, bushy-tailed
critters kept busy collecting snacks to sell.

Preparations were coming together just fine
in the dusty arena.
Rowdy Randy buzzed around helping some fuzzy varmints
and winged cowpokes fine-tune their routines.

"Act big and dare to be mighty!"
Randy reminded the contestants.

Rowdy Randy was a born leader,
and she knew exactly who she was,
a fearless legend.
But she felt like something just wasn't right.
"Must be pre-show jitters,"
she told herself,
and shook that suspicion right off.

Production was moving along, and it was time
for Randy's loyal sidekick,
Ronnie the jackalope, to spread the word.

Ronnie filled his mailbag with posters and postcards.
Then lickety-split, he took off like the chinook wind.

He raced from the rugged Rockies
to the picturesque Pacific.
His elusiveness and quick movements made him
the perfect Jackrabbit Express.

Rowdy Randy was a legend to behold,
and curious critters from every crick, cave, and tree stump
were ready for their own firsthand stories
to pass on to those unlucky enough to stay behind.

Friends and family packed up
for the long adventure
across the rough terrain.
Swimming holes broke up the day,
and campfire gatherings
carried stories into the night.

Some families rode in bustling covered wagons.
Those traveling by stagecoach thought they were riding in style.

"Well, ain't this a sight to see!" Rowdy Randy thought
when crowds of critters began to arrive.

Finally! It was time for the Wild West Show to begin.
The fierce, burrow-digging dudes
were the ticket and entrance security.
They were ready to stop any trouble in its tracks.

Excited spectators scurried to their seats.
The concession crew wove in and out of the crowd,
shouting, "Peanuts, honey sticks, buffalo berries!"

The large-hoofed outlaws bugled
their best show opening tune.
Rowdy Randy was the
ringleader and the main
spokesfly for the night.

The starting event was the obstacle course.
The teeny, tiny acrobatic outlaw
could move in any direction at a moment's notice,
including upside down!

She was exotic in her colorful flair and flashy movements.
Her marksmanship was unmatched.

The audience couldn't believe the furry-footed fellow could
outclimb the lively, mouthful-of-nuts buckaroo.

"What a great start to a first show!" Rowdy Randy said.

But she wondered why
she couldn't shake that foreboding feeling
she had from the start.
Maybe someone didn't pay their entrance fee,
she thought.
But she laughed it off and walked
through the crowd,
shaking hands with her fans.

The fanciest and fastest rope stunts were led
by the eight-legged artists.

No one could outdo the speedy,
sharp-visioned aerialist in speed or skill.

The audience was on the edge of their seats
during the high jump, and they held their breath
when the critters walked the tightrope.

The audience cheered!
Howling, buzzing, and rattle shaking.

The day's events had kept everyone entertained.
There would be stories for centuries!

The flaming glow of the sunset against the split boulders was the
sign that the grand finale was soon to come.

Rowdy Randy looked sharp in her new leathers
and shiny new cowgirl hat. She was ready to shock the audience,
hoping her excitement was what was stirring up
her strange feeling that there was a shadow looming.

A true showfly, she steadied her thoughts.
"Time for action, to dare to be great. Time for
the story of a lifetime!"

The crowd was restless as it grew dark
and twinkling lights appeared. The stage was perfectly set
for the flare and drama Randy desired.

"This final event will deepen my legacy," she said.

A hush fell over the crowd in the large arena.
Every bug and furry fan were as still as a stone.

Then the background sounds started
with a constant drumming, slow and low, followed by
louder and louder screeches and stomps.

From the shadows a large beast appeared.
And there she was, daredevil Rowdy Randy,
standing taller than a ten-gallon hat.

The crowd was speechless. No chirps. No grunts.
Nothing but eyes as big as full moons.
Could Randy really be on top
of this dangerous desperado? The brute stared
down the crowd and gave a snort.

What a Wild West Show! Rowdy Randy
tipped her hat and bowed. The crowd
went wild, whistling and whooping.

Whoopee ti yi yo! What a grand show!

The evening stars danced across the night sky,
and it was time for the travelers to head home
on the windswept prairies.

The legend of Rowdy Randy had been seen firsthand.
The tall tales would last long after the stage
had been swept and the last banner had been put away.

The show had been a success,
but why did Rowdy Randy still have
that uneasy feeling?

She noticed something—
or someone—in the distance.

Rowdy Randy suddenly stopped cold.
That shadow feeling
she'd been sensing all day
was no shadow at all.
Who was this sneaky scoundrel?

"That'll be the day,"
Rowdy Randy grumbled.

CASEY DAY RISLOV has been to many rodeos with her family and watched her two sons, her own daring duo, compete in activities at the local Wyoming rodeo. Casey loves bringing the wild west to schools during her popular author visits where the students get rowdy with Randy, hollering "yeehaw!" during the bucking horned lizard scene in *Rowdy Randy*, the first book in the Rowdy Randy series. Find all of Casey's books at caseyrislovbooks.com.

ZACHARY PULLEN'S picture-book illustrations have won awards and garnered starred reviews. He has been honored several times with acceptance into the prestigious Society of Illustrator juried shows and the Communication Arts: Illustration Annual, best in current illustration. Zak lives under the big blue skies of Wyoming with his wife Renate and their son Hudson. See more of his work at zacharypullen.com.